# Delilah digs for
# TREASURE

## Rachel Pank

# BLue Bananas

For Mum

# Delilah digs for TREASURE

## Rachel Pank

MAMMOTH

## Titles in the series:

First published in Great Britain 1997
by Heinemann and Mammoth, imprints of Reed International Books Ltd
Michelin House, 81 Fulham Road, London SW3 6RB
and Auckland, Melbourne, Singapore and Toronto
Text and Illustrations copyright © Rachel Pank 1997
The Author has asserted her moral rights
Paperback ISBN 0 7497 2632 6
Hardback ISBN 0 434 97463 3
1 3 5 7 9 10 8 6 4 2
A CIP catalogue record for this title
is available from the British Library
Produced by Mandarin Offset Ltd
Printed and bound in China

It was Delilah's birthday.

'I'll take you shopping,' said Grandma.

'So you can choose your present.'

5

They went to a toyshop in town.

There were lots of different

toys to choose from.

Grandma found a pink ballet dress.

'Oh look,' she said,

'it has pink shoes to match.'

'I hate ballet,' said Delilah.

Delilah already knew what she wanted.

'I'd like a spade and a pirate outfit,
please,' she said.

9

Delilah got what she wanted.

It was her birthday after all.

'You look like a proper pirate,' said her mum.

Her baby brother, Tom, liked her pirate hat so much he tried to eat it.

'Hats don't taste nice,' said Grandma.

The next morning, after breakfast, Delilah
fetched her spade to dig for treasure.

'Me dig! Me dig!' said Tom.

'When you're big, you can dig,' said

Delilah. But she let him have her hat.

Delilah went into the garden.

She did a lot of digging.

Lots and . . .

. . . lots of digging.

But all Delilah found were bones.

Big ones and small ones.

14

Soon lots of dogs turned up.

Big ones

and small ones.

'Grrr!'

'Hey!' they said. 'We buried those

bones! That's our treasure.'

'Ooops!' said Delilah. 'Sorry.'

Delilah started to dig somewhere else.

More treasure!

This time she found a store of acorns.

'Mine!' said a small, angry squirrel.

'I'm saving them for later!'

'Oh dear! I didn't know,' said Delilah.

'I'll put them back.'

Delilah took her spade to a

quiet spot, under a shady tree.

After a little digging,

her spade hit

something hard again.

'Treasure!' yelled Delilah.

OUCH!

'Oh, my poor roots,'
groaned the tree.
'Sorry, tree,'
said Delilah.
She put the soil
back carefully.

19

Delilah went indoors for lunch.

All that digging had made her very

hungry. She gobbled up two helpings of

everything. Then she was ready to go

back to her treasure hunt.

Finished already?

Delilah wanted to dig again,

but her spade was missing.

Spade!

Mum helped her to look for it.

She looked on the chairs

and under the sofa.

Delilah emptied her toy box.

She found her spade right at the
bottom, where Tom had buried it.
Tom clapped his hands. He thought
it was very funny.

You'll never be a pirate.

Delilah didn't.

She put on her boots
and stomped crossly out
of the kitchen.

Delilah plodded across the
garden and started to dig. She put
a handful of treasure in her sack.

'Delilah!'
called her mum.
'What are you doing
with my bulbs?'
Delilah had
done it again!

24

She helped her mother put the bulbs back.

Poor Delilah. She was a good digger-upper,

but the treasure she found always

belonged to other people.

Delilah found another empty patch
of earth. She looked around.

This must be
the place!

No tree,

no roots,

no flowers.

Not a dog

or a squirrel

in sight.

She started to dig. She heard a
scrabbling noise. It was Spencer,
her cat. Then Delilah
remembered – it was
Spencer's favourite
spot for...

*you know what!*

'Yucky yuck!' Delilah wailed. She washed her spade under the garden tap. Then she went indoors and scrubbed her hands clean.

Delilah went upstairs and sat on her
bed. 'Did you find any treasure?'
asked Grandma.

'Not today, Grandma,' said Delilah.

Grandma gave her a big hug.

The next day Delilah had to look

very hard for a new place to dig.

There was a patch next
to Tom's sandpit.

Delilah dug hard.

Delilah dug deep.

She saw something shiny.

Thanks, Lilah!

'Well done,' said Dad. 'It's Tom's fire
engine. We thought we'd lost it.'

That weekend, Delilah's dad said: 'We'll go down to the beach. People lose things in the sand. You're sure to find some buried treasure there.'

The sand was easy to dig.

Delilah dug and dug.

Soon there was a huge hole.

But all  Delilah found were three shells,

two pebbles and a baby crab.

Then Tom borrowed her

pebbles and shells to

decorate his sandcastle

and the

crab

scuttled away.

The next day Delilah was sad.

Grandma tried to cheer her up.

'Why don't we go to the museum

and see some treasure?'

'Oh yes!' Delilah cried.

'There'll be real pirates' treasure,

won't there?'

'I expect so,' Grandma smiled.

39

In the museum they saw lots of things

that had been buried for hundreds of

years, until someone had dug them up.

'Those broken cups don't look like proper treasure,' Delilah said.

'Wait until you see this,' said Grandma.

She led Delilah to the next room.

'Look, Grandma!' Delilah cried.
There were gold coins and a beautiful
necklace and ear-rings that once
belonged to a princess.

Real treasure!

On the way home, Grandma asked

Delilah, 'Would you like to dig for

treasure in my garden?'

Delilah's eyes grew wider and wider.

'Treasure?' she whispered.

'In your garden?'

Grandma just smiled.

That afternoon, Delilah could hardly wait for Grandma to show her where to dig. The sun was shining and Delilah felt lucky.

Almost at once Delilah's spade hit something. Could it be Grandma's treasure? Do you know what it was?

Potatoes! Great big tasty potatoes.

Delilah filled her sack. Soon it

was so full she could not lift it.

Grandma came running out to help.

'Well done, Delilah,' she said.

Delilah smiled.

She had her very

own treasure

at last.

And she could eat it too!